DRAGON ACADEMY

Laura Shenton

DRAGON ACADEMY

Laura Shenton

Iridescent Toad Publishing

Iridescent Toad Publishing.

This book is entirely a work of fiction. The names, characters and incidents portrayed in it are the work of the author's imagination. Any resemblance to actual persons, living or dead, events or localities is entirely coincidental.

Designations used by companies to distinguish their products are often claimed as trademarks. All brand names and product names used in this book and on its cover are trade names, service marks, trademarks and registered trademarks of their respective owners. The publishers and the book are not associated with any product or vendor mentioned in this book. None of the companies referenced within the book have endorsed the book.

Cover by Kuro Ishi.

First edition. ISBN: 978-1-913779-86-3

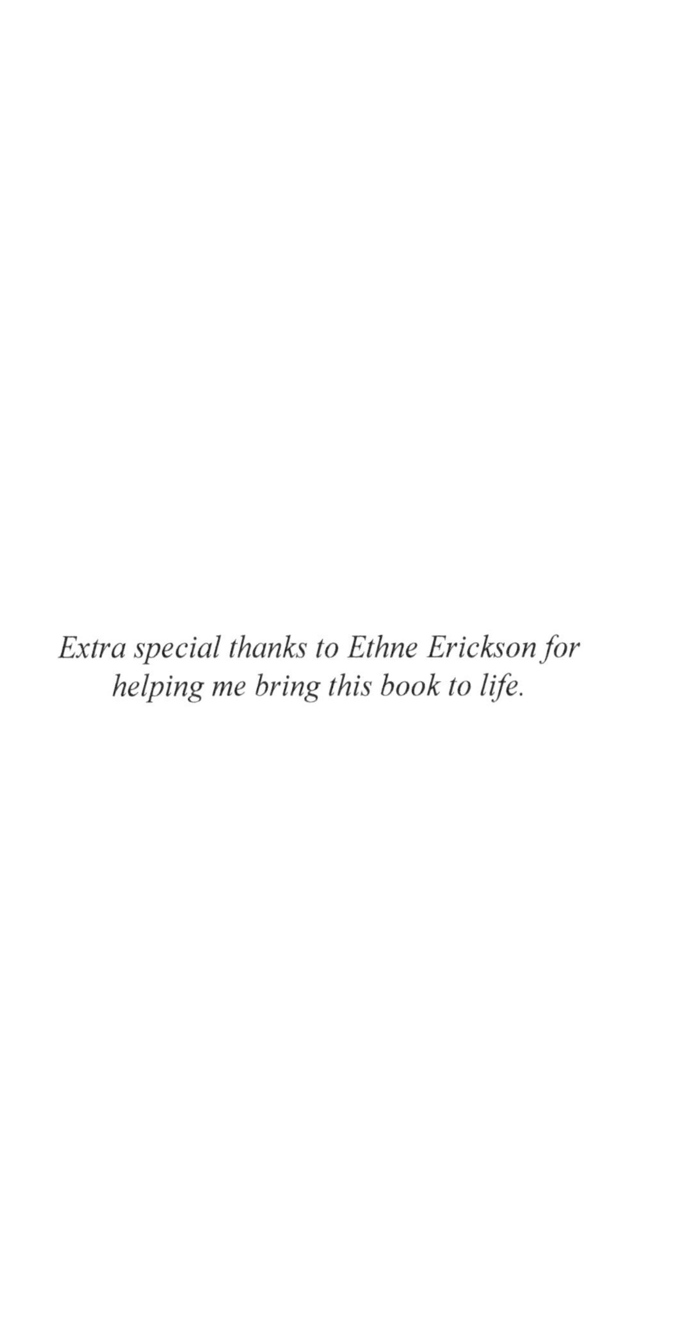

Extra special thanks to Ethne Erickson for helping me bring this book to life.

Chapter One

Her friends wanted a pet dog, but Esme wanted a dragon. People in other villages were allowed to keep dragons as pets, and Esme didn't see why hers had to be any different. Overall, her village held a tremendous hatred towards dragons. Whenever Esme asked her friends, her family, or anyone who would listen, she was always given the same answer.

"It's just the way things are," they would tell her. "Dragons are dangerous, evil beasts."

Despite the insistence of those around her, nobody had ever been able to change Esme's mind.

"Have you ever even seen a dragon?" she asked her father, Declan, as they were sewing new seeds in their fields.

"Don't need to," he replied with a grunt, stooping to pour seeds from his hands to the ground.

"But if you've never seen one, how do you know they're all that bad?" Esme insisted.

Esme's mother, Amethyst, gently touched her on the shoulder.

"Please, dear," she said. "We've been over this so many times before. Do we really need to go over it again?"

"Yes!" Esme exclaimed, exasperated. "We've been over it, but nobody has ever been able to give me a straight answer. I don't think you have one! There's no reason to hate dragons as much as you do. I don't understand it!"

She violently threw a small handful of seeds at the ground.

"There's no need for you to understand it, dear," Amethyst said quietly, sewing her seeds as she walked alongside her daughter. "All you have to do is keep away from dragons. That's all we're asking."

"What if I don't want to stay away from them?" Esme said, voicing her deepest desire. "What if I want to go to the dragon academy in the Harauin town?"

Together, Esme's parents looked up sharply.

"Esme!" said Amethyst, her tone serving as a warning.

"Dragon Academy!?" Esme's father yelled. "That place is for ignorant scum with nowhere else to go! It's for the rejects of this world, to find what solace they can amongst monsters. Dragon Academy is no place for a fine young lady like you! No, Esme. Don't ever speak of this to me again!"

Esme sighed, looking down at the rows of seeds she was scattering.

"Your father only wants what is best for you," said Amethyst, keen to comfort her daughter and to soothe any rising tensions. "So do I."

"How do you know what's best for me?" Esme argued. "I'm a grown woman, Mother. At some point, you're going to have to let me make my own decisions."

"I know," Amethyst said sadly, her expression one of defeat. "When it comes to Dragon Academy though, a decision like that isn't yours to make. That awful place is out of the question. It's up to you what you would like to do with the rest of your life, but Dragon Academy is simply out of the question. Besides, your father and I have been talking about giving you some land to start a farm on, and if you were to get married soon…”

“Mother, I can’t!” Esme sharply interrupted, startling her mother into silence. “I can’t just get married and start a farm. I can’t do what you and Father did! It was wonderful for you. I’m happy for you! But it’s not what I want in my life – and it never will be! You’ve been trying to force this on me since I was a child. It’s not going to work anymore. I’m sorry.”

“Esme, please. Don’t push us away like this. We just want…”

“What’s best for me. I know, Mother. But have you ever considered that Dragon Academy might be what is best for me?” Esme pleaded, desperate for her mother to at least understand her point of view, even if she didn’t agree with it.

“I’m sorry, Esme,” was all Amethyst said.

Esme threw down her sack of seeds. They spilled out onto the ground as a tear trickled down her face.

“I’m taking a break and going for a walk,” she said, abandoning the task at hand, and her parents, in the field.

It wasn't a new argument. In fact, it was an argument that Esme had been having with her parents nearly every day since her eighteenth birthday. Her parents wanted her to settle down and start a farm but, quite simply, she wanted to be free to explore the possibility of dragons. She wanted to dream, to wonder, to muse on the possibility of "what if?". Her parents wanted her to sink back into reality and stay true to, what they believed, were her roots.

She walked the same path every day, knowing the route by heart: through the forest, along the river, circling back through the forest, through the tiny village, and back to the farm that she'd called home for the last twenty-two years. The walks were the only time during which she felt free to be herself; the forest didn't judge her for her love of dragons, and the river was always there to listen.

"They can't even accept the possibility that they might be wrong!" she shouted out into the forest, startling a squirrel. "They have no facts, no logic, no argument! They have nothing, and yet they expect me to accept what they say. How can I?"

She kicked at a rock, falling into a disappointed silence.

The situation felt as though it was the same old

cycle: she'd bring the subject up, they'd shut it down, and then she'd go for a walk, feeling lonely, misunderstood, and miserable.

"Nothing ever changes," she told the wind as it whistled through the trees. "I guess if there was something else to focus on, the situation might not feel so frustrating. There's nothing though – just farming and wishing for more."

Esme sighed, once again falling silent and appreciating the soft rippling of the river up ahead. She loved the sound of water in motion, so much so that she softened her footsteps and held her breath as she approached, not wishing to mask the sound.

As she got closer, she realised that something else was by the river. It had a large, glimmering gold body, with gigantic wings and a fearless face.

A dragon.

Chapter Two

E sme crouched down behind a rock, peeking over it to get a closer look at the dragon. She had seen many dragons fly over her village before, but there was something different about this one. As it sat before her, drinking from the river, she could see every detail of its wings and tail. She could see the light shining off every individual scale. She could see the majesty in its stance, and the wisdom in its eyes.

Esme quietly sat down on the ground. With just her fingers twisting a blade of grass, she remained entirely still otherwise, simply watching the dragon drink from the cold stream of water with its long tongue.

Seeing the powerful-looking creature, she could appreciate why her family feared dragons. She, too, should have been frightened. But she wasn't.

It's just so beautiful. So stunningly beautiful.

Esme wanted to stroke the scales on its neck. She wanted to run her fingers along the fragile membrane of its wings. She wanted to sit on its back and let it carry her far away from her mundane life.

I would be so happy, even if only for a few moments, to fly on the back of a dragon. I wish I could. If only I could have that chance.

As if the dragon had read Esme's mind, it looked up, water dripping from its mouth. Esme watched, not even daring to breathe. She gasped as it met her gaze, its silvery blue eyes staring deeply into her very soul.

Suddenly, almost too quickly to see, the dragon jumped into the sky and spread its wings. Esme gasped at the sudden rush of wind. She abandoned her hiding place behind the rock to run out into the clearing, fixated on the sky as her eyes followed the dragon. It flew higher and higher until it vanished behind the clouds.

Esme watched the sky longingly, hoping so much that the dragon would soon return. When it didn't, she lowered her head to look back down to the ground.

I can't stay here. I just can't do it anymore.

The simple life of a farmer would stifle her. She was sure of it.

If I could get to Dragon Academy, I could learn how to ride a dragon. They seem like such wonderful creatures to be around. I could make it my life's mission to do right by them. Not only would it be better than the life I have now, but the thought of taking that first step just feels so right.

Esme sighed and started to walk down the path leading back to the village. She had toyed with the idea of going to Dragon Academy, many times before, but had never reached the point of following it up.

What's stopping me?

Deciding that it was time to be honest with herself, she knew that deep down, it was fear that was stopping her. In leaving the village to go to the academy, her parents would probably disown her. Everything she had ever known would be lost; she would have to fend for herself and build a new life entirely.

Maybe that wouldn't be such a bad thing. Maybe I could do it, out there on my own!

But that tiny voice of doubt still echoed in Esme's mind.

What if you can't? What if you fail, and have no home to come back to? What if you go to the academy and end up hating it? What if the life you have now is too good to put on the line?

When she closed her eyes and thought of the dragon, Esme knew. She wouldn't regret leaving. She wouldn't miss the farmer's life. She would be content, happy, and free.

She just had to believe and take a leap of faith.

Chapter Three

"Esme, darling, can you pass the butter?"

Esme did so without looking at her mother.

Tell them. Tell them you're leaving!

"Amethyst, dear, did you hear?" Esme's father asked her mother. "There was another dragon sighting."

"No?!" Amethyst exclaimed. "Surely not?! That's the third one this week!"

"Really?" Esme asked.

It was the first she had heard of other dragon sightings in quite a while.

Sensing her daughter's excitement, Amethyst chose to ignore it and turned to continue the conversation with her husband.

"Did they kill this one?"

"No," Declan answered. "The ugly monster got away."

"They're not monsters," Esme muttered.

Amethyst glared at her daughter before continuing to ignore her.

"Declan, do you think we're safe here?"

"I should think so, sweetheart," he replied. "The last time a dragon attacked the village was a very long time ago."

"Maybe that's because dragons aren't dangerous and don't want to hurt anyone," Esme said, speaking a bit louder than before.

"Do you have something to say, Esme?" her father demanded.

Tell them!

She took a deep breath.

"I've decided that I *will* be going to Dragon Academy."

Amethyst froze, staring at Esme in shock. Declan scowled.

"No, you're not," he said.

"Yes, I am," Esme insisted.

"No, you're not!" he retorted, raising his voice. "We've been over this. Dragon Academy is for ignorant scum with nowhere else to go! Dragon Academy is for the rejects of this planet to find what solace they can amongst monsters! Dragon Academy…"

"Is no place for a lady. Blah, blah, blah!" Esme interrupted, raising her voice to match her father's. "But you don't really know that, do you? You've never been there!"

"Don't raise your voice to me, young lady!"

"You never listen. So now, *I'm* going to stop listening. I'm packing my things and leaving at first light," Esme said finally, confident in her decision.

"If you do that, you will never be welcome here again," her father said darkly.

"Good," Esme snapped, walking away to her

bedroom.

She quickly began packing her things into a leather satchel. There wasn't much that she needed to take with her – just a couple of changes of clothes and footwear, one of her favourite books, and some survival supplies. Hearing her parents arguing downstairs made her feel guilty, especially when her mother started crying. Esme firmly reminded herself that having got this far, it wasn't the time to back out.

I have to leave. Otherwise, I will be stuck here for the rest of my life. I can't be stuck here, I just can't! If I don't leave now, I will never find the courage to do so.

She had only just finished packing her things when she heard someone knocking on her bedroom door. It was her mother, with tear-filled eyes and a quivering lip.

"Esme, I beg of you. *Please* don't do this. Stay here, with your father and me. He is adamant about you not leaving! He *will* disown you, and I… I'll never see you again!"

Amethyst burst into a fresh round of tears and hugged her daughter tightly. Esme held her mother for what would surely be the last time. Then, she pulled away, even more determined.

"Please don't leave," Amethyst implored, her voice barely a whisper as she looked desperately into Esme's eyes.

"I'm sorry, but I have to," Esme said earnestly.

"But I don't understand," said Amethyst.

"I know you don't," Esme replied. "Neither of you do! And that's the problem. I *have* to find people who understand my love of dragons. People who understand *me*."

With that, having decided not to wait until the morning to start off on her journey, Esme grabbed her bag of supplies. She brushed past her mother and charged down into the kitchen, where she filled up a flask with water and put it in her bag.

Her father was there, standing and staring at her.

"Can I take some food with me?" Esme asked.

A look of deep sadness flashed in her father's eyes, but he stepped aside.

"Declan, do something!" Amethyst pleaded.

"There's bread in the pantry," Declan said coldly.

"Thank you, Father," Esme replied.

Aware that she may never see her family again, Esme determined that she was going to be as gentle – and as dignified – as she could be in the circumstances. She took only the food that she would need, putting it in her bag along with her other supplies.

"Goodbye, Mother. Goodbye, Father," she said quietly. "I wish you all the best."

As Amethyst began crying harder, Declan put his arm around her.

"I hope you find what you're looking for, Esme," he said stoically.

With that, Esme walked outside and quietly closed the front door, leaving her old life behind.

Chapter Four

Esme walked all night. She passed through her village, and then the forest, stopping only for a moment at the river where she had seen the dragon. From there, she followed the main road, which would lead her to the next village and eventually, to the town of Harauin – the location of Dragon Academy.

By sunrise, Esme was tired, hungry, and sore. She walked until she found a rock big enough to sit on. Allowing herself to rest there for a while, she ate some of the bread that she had brought with her. Although her feet ached, she was making good time.

At this rate, I should be able to reach the academy before sunset, and then I'll start my new life! Not bad going, for my first day on my own!

The thought energised her. She smiled and then took a final sip of water before wrapping up what was left of the bread to put back in her bag.

"You can do this," she told herself.

And with that, she was back on the road again. It wasn't until a good few hours later, when she could see the town on the horizon, that the reality of the situation hit her.

Can I just walk into the academy? Will they let me in? Is there an application process?

It suddenly dawned on Esme that all she truly knew about the academy was born out of rumours. Although she had thought about it many times before, she hadn't made a solid plan of approach.

Don't panic, Esme. Take this one step at a time. First, find a place to stay for the night. The sun is already going down. You'll need a good sleep, and then in the morning, you can figure out a plan.

She walked into the first inn that she spotted in the town. A bustling pub with rooms above the main restaurant, it was full of people, talking and laughing. Many of the patrons seemed to be there on business. It was in stark contrast to the quiet places that she was used to.

"How much for a room for the night?" she asked

the man behind the bar.

"Ten coins for a private room, five for a shared one," he answered, wiping a glass with a cloth.

"Shared?" Esme questioned, mentally counting the coins she had taken from her savings.

"You can share a room with someone," he said. "Two single beds to a room."

You don't have much money, Esme. You should try to save it wherever possible. But what if you get paired with someone you don't like?

"Who would I share with?" Esme asked.

The man nodded to a young woman who was sitting with a sandwich at a table by the window.

"She asked for a shared room," he said. "Maybe you'd like to share with her."

"I'll go and ask if she wants to share with me," Esme replied. "Thank you."

"Of course. Let me know what you decide to do," the man said, turning to take an order from someone else.

Esme took a deep breath and walked up to the woman. She looked as though she was also in her early-twenties, with wispy silver hair and contented blue eyes.

"Hello," said Esme.

"Hello!" the woman replied warmly, smiling as she looked up from her sandwich. "How are you?"

"I am well. The man at the bar said you're interested in sharing a room?"

"That's right! Are you interested in sharing one with me? I'll be very quiet, and I'll keep to myself."

"Yes, if you wouldn't mind sharing one with me," Esme said, returning the woman's smile. "I'll be quiet too! I've had a long journey and I only wish to sleep."

"Have you?" the woman asked cheerily. "Sit down, sit down, it's not time for bed yet. Tell me, who are you? Where have you come from?"

Esme sat down at the other side of the table.

"Would you like something to eat?" the woman asked. "My treat!"

"Really?" Esme asked hesitantly.

"Yes, of course! You look hungry, and I have to thank you for splitting the cost of a room with me!" the woman said as she waived across the room to get the attention of a waiter. "I'm Finley, but everyone calls me Finn. What's your name?"

"I'm Esme. Nice to meet you."

"The pleasure is mine! Do you know what you want to eat?"

Esme scanned the menu reluctantly.

"It's ok," said Finn, patient and understanding. "We'll try some of everything and see what you like!"

She then turned to the waiter – who had just arrived – and started reeling off a list of various dishes. Esme was surprised and rather shocked. The food wasn't cheap.

Unable to ignore Esme's expression, once the waiter had left, Finn proceeded to explain.

"My father is kind of a big deal," she said, tucking some hair behind her ear. "Not to brag or anything, but the cook here is always happy to prepare more than a few extras for me."

"What does your father do?" Esme asked.

"He's headmaster at Dragon Academy. It's up the road from here."

"Seriously?!" Esme exclaimed, her eyes widening.

"Yeah, why?" Finn asked, raising an eyebrow suspiciously.

Esme sat in silent shock for a moment.

"Are you ok?" Finn finally asked.

"I'm on my way to Dragon Academy! I've always wanted to go! It's why I'm in town!" Esme explained excitedly. "I've travelled here from my village."

"No way?!" Finn enthused, a huge smile spreading across her face. "What a coincidence! This is awesome! We can study together!"

"I hope so!" Esme replied, her tone changing to a serious one. "Do you know how I can apply? Do they have a screening process, or something like that?"

"You don't know?"

Esme shook her head in embarrassment, but Finn waved her hand as if to wave away the shame.

"Don't worry about it!" Finn insisted. "I'll talk to my father, and we'll get you in. Usually, there is an application process, but I'm sure we can get around that. I can see that you are fully dedicated to this. Do you have money for tuition?"

Her hopes sliding away, Esme stared down at the table as she shook her head. Finn reached out to touch her hand comfortingly.

"Hey, hey, don't worry about it! We'll sort something out," she said reassuringly. "We'll get you into the academy, I promise! We'll sleep here tonight. Tomorrow, we'll go and talk to my father."

"Thank you," Esme said humbly, not quite sure how to express her gratitude.

"You're welcome."

"I have to ask though," said Esme, still astounded at what was being offered. "You must live around here?"

"Yes," said Finn, taking a sip of her drink.

"So, why are you staying at an inn?"

"Whenever my parents entertain, I like to come here. Father is holding a board meeting – or something like that. Staying at the inn saves me the bother of a painfully boring evening with a bunch of stuffy diplomats."

As Finn was speaking, the waiter came by with a large tray of food and beverages. Esme's eyes widened as she saw the array of variety before her.

"To new friends," she said happily, raising her glass for a toast.

"To new friends!" Finn replied, raising her glass in kind.

New friends, and a new life.

Chapter Five

Once they had settled into their room, Esme and Finn stayed up into the small hours, talking about all kinds of things. Finn spoke of how she had grown up around dragons. Her mother and father both worked for Dragon Academy – her father as headmaster, and her mother as an administrator. She told Esme magical stories about graduates of the academy, who had left to go on glorious adventures with their dragons.

"I had never thought about it that way," Esme said, staring up at the ceiling in her bed that night.

"What's that?" Finn asked from her bed across the room.

"I had never actually thought that I would get my own dragon," Esme said, sleepy and happy. "Just to be around them would be enough."

"You're going to see them and be around them

every day!" Finn explained, laughing endearingly. "Several live at the academy – like pets. The bigger ones are kept in the stables, but we can go and see them every day if you want to."

"Really?" Esme asked, her face a picture of joy.

After having felt obliged to lower her expectations for so long, it all sounded too wonderful to be true!

"Of course!" Finn said, beaming at her friend's contagious happiness.

"Have you got your own dragon?" Esme asked.

"Not yet," said Finn. "Father doesn't want it to seem as though he's giving me special preference over the other students. A lot of my friends have already been assigned their dragons, so it will be nice to hang out with someone else who is still waiting for theirs."

Esme sensed that Finn had a need to take her under her wing.

"We should get some sleep," Finn said thoughtfully. "You need to get some rest so that tomorrow, we can introduce you to the academy!"

With that, Finn and Esme settled down to go to

sleep. Esme didn't fall asleep right away though. She stayed up for a little while, enjoying the feeling of complete freedom and total happiness.

Maybe things will work out after all.

***

Before Esme knew it, somebody was shaking her awake.

"Esme! Get up!"

"Five more minutes, Mother," she mumbled, rolling over and pulling the duvet over her head.

Esme groaned. In her half-asleep state, she thought she was back with her family at the farm.

"Esme!" Finn said, bursting into laughter. "I'm not your mother!"

Esme sat up and wiped the sleep from her eyes.

"Good morning!" Finn said cheerily, having composed herself. "Come on, get up and get dressed! We'll have breakfast, and then we'll head off to the academy!"

"The academy!" Esme repeated, finally having

gathered her bearings.

"Yes. Come on!"

Esme jumped out of bed and got dressed into a spare set of clothes that she had brought with her from home. Ready in less than five minutes, she followed Finn downstairs for breakfast.

"I've already ordered some pancakes for you," said Finn. "Does that sound good?"

Esme nodded eagerly.

"Awesome!" Finn said. "I'm so excited to show you around the academy today! You're going to love it!"

With the beautifully prepared breakfasts in front of them at the table, Esme was too excited to eat very much.

"We'll head over to the academy straight after breakfast," Finn said, her mouth full of pancakes. "We'll head straight to my father's office. I'll talk to him, and we'll get you enrolled. After that, I can show you around. You don't have a place to stay in town, do you? I don't remember you mentioning it."

Esme shook her head, a worried expression crossing her face.

"Don't worry about it," Finn said quickly. "The academy has plenty of rooms for students and staff who can't – or don't want to – find a place in town. Some of the students and staff choose to live in the town; they prefer to have a break from being around dragons all the time – dragons can be loud at night."

"I won't mind," Esme said. "I want to be around dragons all the time. Besides, I'm used to noise at night. It comes with having lived on a farm for so long."

"That's great!" said Finn, tapping the end of her fork thoughtfully on the table. "It won't be hard to find you a room."

"I hope it's not too expensive," Esme said honestly.

"We'll work it out with my father," Finn said firmly. "Are you ready to go?"

Esme nodded and the two friends stood up to leave. They paid the innkeeper and then walked outside into the town.

With Esme following closely behind, Finn led the

way through the bustling streets. She was almost a little too slow for Esme, who had no desire to look in the shop windows, speak to the vendors, and take in the sights. Although it was all exciting, and although she had never seen anything like it before, Esme was bursting to see the academy.

"We'll be there soon!" Finn said reassuringly, sensing Esme's feeling of urgency.

As they walked through more of the town, Finn told Esme about some of the landmarks as they passed them.

"That's the bookstore, there. Mrs Finnigan owns it. She's super nice. She'll let you just sit in there and read, even if you don't want to buy anything. Mr Eric owns that store, there. He sells everything. If you need any outdoor supplies, go there. If he doesn't have it, no one will! Oh, and those are apartments! A lot of students who go to the academy, they live there. The room on the very top is Marcy's, you'll see it eventually. She throws the greatest parties!"

"Where is the academy?" Esme asked after a while.

"It's right on the edge of town. Out by the cliffs," Finn explained. "It was built on the cliffs so that dragons can come and go with ease. The basement goes down into the cliffs themselves, where there are doors for the dragons to push open. It's great for if they want to simply drop down into flight. It saves them the struggle of having to take off from the ground, especially when carrying an inexperienced rider, you know?"

"I didn't know that," Esme whispered, amazed.

"Yeah. Whoever built the academy really knew what they were doing."

"Who built it?"

"I don't think anyone really knows. It's hundreds of years old. My grandparents studied there. They just felt so drawn towards dragons, and the academy's instructors taught them how to harness that feeling into a powerful bond."

"How did anyone first work out how to communicate with dragons?" Esme asked, fascinated.

"I'd like to think that the dragons taught them," Finn said with a smile. "But no one really knows. I wish there was a way to find out, but I guess we'll never know."

"Oh," said Esme, trying to take it all in.

I've got a lot to learn...

Chapter Six

Esme and Finn had finally arrived at the gates of Dragon Academy. It was huge compared to what Esme had been expecting. Behind the tall iron bars was a large, old building, with several smaller buildings attached to it.

The sea breeze whipped through Esme's hair, and felt like tiny icicles tapping at her cheeks. It reminded her of how she had only seen the sea once before – as a child when her family had taken a trip to the beach. The beach she had visited all those years ago was nothing like the churning sea that was beyond the cliffs of the academy, with waves crashing aggressively.

"The constant sound of the ocean takes some getting used to!" Finn shouted above the noise. "If you can believe this, I sometimes find it rather relaxing! I promise it's quiet inside though."

Esme nodded as Finn pushed on the huge gate blocking the path to the academy. As it slowly opened, it sounded as though the hinges were in need of oil.

"There's usually a dragon on guard at the gate, but with it being the weekend, there's nobody around at the moment," said Finn. "The dragons need a day off, just as much as the rest of us do."

As they walked up the pathway towards the main building, Esme stared in awe. It was like a large mansion, and then some.

"They've added a couple of rooms over the years," Finn explained. "Oh, and you see those platforms out to the side? They serve as an excellent launch point for riders who are becoming more confident on their dragons."

The thought of flying on a dragon had crossed Esme's mind many times before, but she had never expected that one day, it would become a reality.

I'm going to fly!

Finn walked up the stone steps to the front door, and confidently rang the bell. A few steps behind, Esme stared up at the large building in front of them.

Finn took a step back as the door was yanked open by a girl with blonde hair, who looked to be no older than sixteen. She greeted Finn with a huge smile.

"Hey, Finn!" she said. "Who's your friend?"

"Esme, this is Cassie. She's the little sister of one of our teachers here at the academy. In a year or two, she'll be an official student!"

Cassie nodded, completely unfazed by Finn's description of her.

"Cassie, this is Esme. Once I've convinced Father of it, she's going to be a student here," Finn said confidently.

"So happy to have you here, Esme!" said Cassie. "Come in, come in!"

Esme walked into the main hall of the academy. With its high ceilings and tall stained-glass windows adorned with colourful, majestic dragons, the building looked even bigger on the inside. The staircase in front of Esme looked as though it went up forever. She didn't have time to stare at it for long.

Finn grabbed her hand and pulled her into the first

room on the right. It was an office. Scented with cedarwood and oranges, it was proudly decorated with an oceanic theme. Model ships lined the shelves, and framed drawings of sailors and dragons covered the walls. On the floor was a deep blue carpet. Esme wanted to take her shoes off and bury her toes in the rich, soft material, but decided against the idea. She wanted to make a good first impression.

Towards the back of the office was a smaller room, in which there was a large mahogany desk. Behind it, sat a gentleman who looked to be in his mid-fifties. He was staring through a pair of wide-rimmed glasses at something written on a piece of paper.

"Father?" Finn said, lowering her voice respectfully.

He held up a finger, silently asking her to wait. Esme was fine with the turn of events. It gave her a chance to look around the room. There were two large windows: one overlooking the cliffs, and the other revealing the vast sea. The warming glow coming from the fireplace gave the room a familiar, comforting feel.

Finally, Finn's father looked up.

"What can I do for you?" he asked his daughter, his tone friendly and approachable.

"Father, this is Esme. Esme, this is my father, Grayson Osgood, the headmaster here at the academy."

Following Finn's lead, Esme moved to stand closer to the desk.

"Hello Sir," Esme said quietly, feeling out-of-place and awkward.

"It's nice to meet you!" Headmaster Osgood replied.

He seemed genuine and welcoming, which served to help Esme feel more at ease.

"Esme wants to be a student here, Father," Finn said.

"Does she?" he enquired with an extent of uncertainty. "Have you applied to attend, Esme?"

Esme shook her head and opened her mouth to respond, but Finn quickly began to speak on her behalf.

"She hasn't, but she's come a long way, and has

given up everything to be here. Also, she's a friend of mine. Please, Father, can't she stay?"

"Do you love dragons, Esme? Do you wish to serve them?" he asked as he carefully regarded her cautious expression. "That's what we learn here at Dragon Academy. Other places try to force dragons to serve humans. Here, we learn to serve them, and, in that way, we grow close enough to them that everyone benefits – the dragons included. Do you understand?"

Esme nodded seriously.

"Yes Sir," she replied. "I understand. I will do whatever it takes. I want to learn. And I do love dragons. I've loved dragons for so many years."

Esme had more to say. She had a whole speech planned out in her head. Headmaster Osgood had apparently heard enough though.

"Can you pay for room and board?" he asked.

"No Sir," Esme answered honestly. "I'm afraid I have very little money."

"Are you willing to work around the building to pay for your room and board?" he asked.

There was no judgment in his tone, no hostility. It was a genuine question asked by a kind man, and Esme knew that. She nodded eagerly.

"I'm happy to work, Sir," she confirmed. "I'm a hard worker, and a fast learner. Anything you want me to do, I will do it."

"Excellent," he said. "That's settled then. I can see that you have a genuine passion, and that you want to give this your all. The academy is always keen to support students who will be an asset to what we stand for here."

"Can she board with me?" Finn asked, her face lighting up in excitement.

"Are you sure you don't mind?" Headmaster Osgood asked his daughter.

"Not at all!" Finn said, grabbing Esme's hand in delight.

"Why don't you take Esme up to her room, Finn?" he suggested.

"Thank you, Father, thank you so much!" Finn exclaimed, already pulling Esme away from the desk and towards the door of the office.

Before Finn could pull her out of the room entirely, Esme managed to stand her ground.

"Thank you, Headmaster Osgood," she said humbly. "I promise to embrace this opportunity for all that it's worth. It means a lot to me."

He nodded and smiled at her sincerely.

Chapter Seven

Finn's room was on one of the top floors. It was so high up that Esme was gasping for breath after the climb up the stairs.

"It's definitely a workout," Finn said, panting as well. "But you'll get used to it eventually. At least, that's what the teachers say. Mind you, their rooms are closer to the ground floor, and they rarely come up here. Anyway, we're here now."

The door to Finn's bedroom was painted bright green, displaying a plaque with her name in pink, swirly letters.

"We'll have to add your name to this," she said happily as she pointed to it.

Esme merely nodded and followed Finn inside.

One half of the room was painted white, with bold red patterns of dragons dancing across the walls.

The other half was painted to look like a jungle with trees and vines, the busy design making the rest of the room appear more elegant. Each with a single bed, both sides looked homely.

"With most of the bedrooms here being for two people, two different designs are used to split the space in half," Finn explained. "I've been here for so long that I've had this room to myself for a while, but I'm happy to share it with you! I hope you don't mind, but I'll stick to the jungle side."

"I don't mind at all," Esme said with a genuine smile.

"Perfect! If there's anything else you need, we could pop into town another day. Is that ok with you?"

"Of course," said Esme. "Thank you. Is there any work I need to do today? Who should I talk to about what to do next? Do I need to sign up for a particular set of classes?"

Finn plopped down on her bed, which was covered in books and clothes.

"Don't worry about that for now," she said. "Just relax and settle in. It will be time for dinner soon. I can show you around on the way. Tomorrow will be your first day of classes."

Esme nodded, relieved that she would get the answers she was looking for soon enough. After stretching and yawning, Finn rolled over to hug a large pillow.

"Let me nap for five minutes," she said through another yawn. "Wake me up when they ring the bell for dinner."

With Finn needing a rest, it was the perfect opportunity for Esme to make herself at home. She put her bag down at the foot of her bed, and then moved to look out of the window. She could see the town in the distance. Observing the road upon which she and Finn had walked, it reminded her of how far she had travelled, causing her to wonder about her family.

Don't think about them, Esme. Don't miss them. You're here! You've made it! Finally! You can be happy now!

But Esme didn't feel happy. She missed her family desperately.

You should do something to distract yourself. Make yourself useful. If you're going to stay here, you need to pull your own weight. You need to go above and beyond what they expect. You need to show them that you deserve to be here.

Determined, Esme turned away from the window. She slipped quietly out of the bedroom, leaving Finn to snore softly and get some rest.

Alone in the academy, Esme took a deep breath, taking in the musty smell of old books. After walking down several flights of stairs, she noticed the most delicious scent of baking. Following it, she ended up on a floor with an array of beautiful stained-glass windows – more than she had seen in the main hall, and larger too. There were so many different colours on the windows that the sunbeams from outside made rainbow patterns on the wooden floor.

"Hello there!"

The voice startled Esme, but she soon felt at ease when she saw who it belonged to: a plump, elderly gentleman wearing a food-stained apron. With a bowl of dough in his hands, he was clearly the cook for the academy. He stepped forward and nodded, a friendly twinkle in his eye.

"I'm Felix," he said. "I don't think I've seen you before."

"I'm Esme. I'm a new student. I need a job to pay for my place here."

"When did you get here?" Felix asked with a raised eyebrow.

"Today."

"Ah! So Mrs Fringle hasn't had a chance to get her claws into you."

"Who?" Esme asked, blinking in confusion.

"She usually makes students such as yourself do menial tasks around the academy. A mean old spinster, that one. Tell me, can you bake?"

Esme nodded silently, anxious at the thought of Mrs Fringle.

"Ok," Felix said kindly. "You can work with me. You can help me in the kitchen – before and after mealtimes. Unless, that is, you don't want to help an old man like me, and you'd rather be dusting under Mrs Fringle's watchful eye?"

"I'd love to work with you!" Esme said eagerly.

Felix laughed a jolly laugh that made Esme smile. He formally shook her hand with his free one before passing her the bowl of dough that he'd been cradling.

"Welcome to the kitchen," he said. "Let's make the bread for dinner."

Esme followed him towards the large pantry, determined to work hard.

Chapter Eight

Finn was delighted to hear of Esme's job in the kitchen.

"We can sneak down and get snacks at night, Esme," she said mischievously. "And you can smuggle leftovers up to the room!"

"Great minds think alike," Esme said cheekily as she showed Finn some baked goods wrapped in a cloth napkin.

Finn's eyes sparkled as she hurried to make sure the door of their bedroom was closed.

"The bread turned out well," said Esme, proud of how she had managed to hold her own in working alongside Felix. "There was some left over and…"

Finn waved Esme's explanation away as she delved excitedly into the food.

"I'm glad you'll be working with Felix," she said through a mouthful of bread. "He will make sure you have plenty of free time when you need it. He's good like that."

"I guess I'm lucky to have met him in the hallway," said Esme. "Anyway, let's save some of this bread for later. There's a lovely casserole for dinner and it would be a shame to miss out on it."

***

After a satisfying dinner and a small evening walk around just a fraction of the large building, Esme and Finn retired to their room.

"We'd better get some sleep," said Finn. "You'll need plenty of energy for tomorrow! It will be a busy first day."

Esme nodded and climbed into bed, pulling the duvet over her shoulders as she closed her eyes.

This is perfect.

She couldn't remember having fallen asleep. The next thing she knew, Finn was shaking her awake, and the bell was ringing.

"Wake up! That's the bell for breakfast! We're

going to be late!"

Esme stumbled out of bed, still half asleep. Finn thrust a bundle of clothes into her hands, which turned out to be a navy-blue uniform consisting of a skirt and thick tights, a tie and woollen jumper, and a white, long-sleeved button-up shirt. Esme got dressed as quickly as she could. She then slipped her feet into the smart shoes that she had brought with her, briefly stopping in front of the mirror to fix her hair.

As the pair ran down the stairs, Esme saw lots of other students. Most of them appeared to be in their twenties. They all had the same sleepy, yet focused, looks on their faces.

And these are just some of the students who board here!

"I'll introduce you to more people at breakfast," Finn said happily.

"I should check to see if Felix needs any help in the kitchen first," Esme replied.

Finn hesitated, not wanting to be separated from her friend, but after a moment, she nodded.

"Ok. I'll catch up with you later. Either in the

dining room or, if not, Felix will point you in the right direction."

With that, Finn ran off, leaving Esme to wonder where to go for her first class. She shrugged and decided to ask Felix about it.

The kitchen was messy, hot and smoky. Felix stood over a stovetop that had all the burners on. He was making a huge stack of pancakes with one hand, and scrambled eggs with the other. The remaining burners were occupied with bacon and black pudding. As she observed the inviting offering, Esme's mouth began to water.

"Oops!" Felix exclaimed.

A whole egg slipped out of his hand, but Esme was quick, and she caught it before it could break on the ground. Then, she cracked it on the side of a pan, pouring the contents in with the rest of the scrambled eggs.

"Esme!" Felix said, relieved to have her there to help. "I was wondering if I would see you!"

"I slept a little later than I would usually," she apologised.

"You are forgiven. It was your first night here, after

all! Going forward, we shall have to talk about you getting up a little earlier to help me prepare breakfast."

"I will," said Esme. "Gladly. I'm used to getting up early. I grew up on a farm."

"Did you? Here, why don't you flip those pieces of bacon over and tell me all about it."

Esme told Felix the story of her life while she flipped bacon, then black pudding, then pancakes. While they stacked the food on plates and poured a generous helping of syrup over the pancakes, Felix told Esme about what had brought him to the academy.

"When I was a boy, a dragon saved my life," he said seriously. "My family took me swimming one day and I nearly drowned in the sea. The current was too strong for a young lad. I'm sure that if that big beast hadn't carried me to the shore, I would have perished that day. My parents were terrified – not just because they thought I was going to drown, but of the dragon too! It let me ride on its back. I remember feeling very tall on its smooth, scaly shoulders. It put me down on the sand, and that was that. It was lost to the ocean once again. I'll never know why it chose to save me. I'd like to think that it had a family of its own. After that, I decided to dedicate my life to helping dragons in any way I could. And I just so happen to be a good cook!"

"That's amazing!" Esme said, her eyes shining. "To get so close to a dragon must have been a wonderful experience. And to ride one? I can't even imagine!"

"You'd better start imagining! Learning to ride a dragon is a vital part of studying here at Dragon Academy!"

"Wow," Esme replied, awestruck.

"Now, scoot those plates over here a little bit. The students will come by and grab one each. There are drinks outside. If you like, you and I can eat here where it's cosy and warm – unless, of course, you'd rather eat with everyone else."

Esme considered her options. As much as she enjoyed Finn's company, she needed a little break. Although Finn had said that she would introduce her to more people at breakfast, Esme didn't like being the centre of attention.

"I'll eat with you," she told Felix.

"Here you go," he said, thrusting a warm plate into

her hands. "There's plenty left if you want more!"

Esme ate heartily and Felix laughed when she'd cleaned her plate.

"Would you like some more?" he asked.

Esme nodded, and Felix laughed again before serving her some.

"I'm sure there will be other new students around. They just can't get enough of my delicious food!" he bragged jovially.

"I can understand why," Esme said, quick to agree. "Your food is delicious. The pancakes are fluffy, the eggs are perfectly done, and the bacon is crispy."

"Thank you, my dear, thank you!" Felix said humbly, blushing a little. "I have to say, it's lovely having another set of hands in the kitchen! I can't imagine how I ever managed without you!"

"Really?" Esme asked. "I'm still getting used to this kitchen."

"You've been brilliant," he assured.

Suddenly, a loud bell chimed from somewhere

within the academy.

"It's ringing for first period," Felix explained. "Your first class is on the third floor, in the fourth door on the right. And you're going to be late, so hurry! Leave the dishes for me, I'll do them myself. Just be here for lunch!"

There were so many things that Esme wanted to ask Felix. Not only did he have a kind air of wisdom about him, but he seemed to know a lot about dragons too. She didn't want to be late for her first class though.

"Thank you, Felix," she said, already on her way out of the kitchen.

She cleaned herself whilst running up the stairs to the third floor. By the time she got there, she had missed a couple of spots of flour, and her jumper had a syrup stain, but she had tried her best.

Chapter Nine

Esme took a deep breath and opened the door. The classroom was just as timeless as the other rooms in the academy. It had rows of wooden desks and chairs, and a chalkboard at the front. Back home in her village, Esme had always enjoyed school, and had stayed on until the age of sixteen. Although it had been a good few years since she had been in a classroom, it felt strangely familiar.

Most of the students had already taken their seats. Esme looked around nervously, trying to figure out where to sit. Luckily, a familiar face came bounding up to her.

"Hey!" Finn said quickly, sounding out of breath. "I was wondering when Felix would let you go! Listen, this isn't my class. I took it a couple of years ago. Everyone must take it when they start. Meet me in the hallway when it's over. We have second period together."

With that, Esme's whirlwind of a friend had vanished again, leaving her to stare at the rows of seats in bewilderment.

Where should I sit? Shall I sit at the front? Hmm… I don't want the teacher to ask me all the questions though, especially if I don't know the answers! I could sit at the back, but then would people think I'm being antisocial?

Esme was still standing by the door and overthinking the situation, when the teacher, a middle-aged woman, entered the room.

"Good morning, class. I hope you've all had a good… Oh, hello there! You must be our new student. Esme, is it?"

Esme nodded.

"I'm Mrs Francis. I teach Introduction to Dragon Studies. All new students come through this class at one point or another. There's a seat at the back there, next to Florian."

Mrs Francis gestured towards a thin, pale young man sitting at a desk at the back of the room. There was an empty seat next to him. Not wishing to seem rude, Esme nodded and walked over.

"Hey," she said to him before sitting down.

Florian nodded at her, but didn't say anything.

Just be friendly, Esme. Just be friendly.

"Florian is a cool name," she said quietly.

He looked over and smiled at her. He seemed like a genuinely nice person, and a pleasure to be around.

"Alright, class. Let's get started," said Mrs Francis, commanding the attention of everyone in the room. "Now, most of you know this, but we need to go over the basics. First, what qualifies as a dragon?"

"Ugh!" a young woman in front of Esme groaned, putting her head down on her desk. "Everyone knows this already!"

"Hey, I could use a refresher!" Florian said loudly.

He winked kindly at Esme. She smiled gratefully at him, and then did her best to focus on the lesson.

Mrs Francis talked about the different kinds of dragons. Esme was amazed. There were so many different kinds, so many more than she had expected there to be. Mrs Francis gave everyone a notebook, and Esme took very detailed notes. She wrote everything down, and even drew some sketches of the dragons in the paper's margins. At one point, she was so invested in a drawing that she stopped listening to Mrs Francis' voice. That changed when the teacher's tone changed from light and happy, to dark and fearful.

Esme looked up sharply, her eyes wide, as Mrs Francis explained.

"But there are those who do not love dragons as we do. There are those who capture them, treat them as slaves and use them as weapons. Take the Sparkmasters, for instance. They only ride dragons for the purpose of pillaging towns, burning villages, and causing havoc. It is our job here at Dragon Academy to train wise, quick-witted riders who can advocate against the damage done by those such as Sparkmasters."

Esme felt her hand go up, almost of its own accord.

"Yes, Esme?" Mrs Francis asked.

"How can we do that?" Esme asked. "Do we fight them?"

"We do not condone violence here, Esme. We can beat them by being a good example, and…"

"What good does that do?" Esme demanded, cutting Mrs Francis off. "It doesn't sound like it would do anything, especially against violent dragon enslavers."

Esme gasped. Realising that she had probably spoken out of turn, she scrambled to apologise.

"I'm sorry," she said. "I'm just so sad to hear of what some people do to dragons."

All eyes were on Mrs Francis, the whole class eager to hear her response. She took a second to put her thoughts into words, and then nodded.

"It's ok, Esme. It's a good question. Choosing to be a good example might not seem like it does very much, but it is better than violence. In resorting to that, we would have to use dragons for our own means. It would make us no better than the Sparkmasters."

"But what if some dragons would be happy to fight for a good cause?" Esme asked, not wishing to be confrontational, but still not satisfied with the answer. "What if we partnered with those dragons to rescue other dragons from the Sparkmasters? If a dragon agreed to use its fire to help other dragons, would that still be wrong?"

"Violence is always wrong," Mrs Francis said simply.

"But what the Sparkmasters are doing is wrong," Esme insisted. "If we do nothing to stop them, isn't that wrong too? And if violence is the only way to stop them, doesn't that make it right?"

Growing passionate about the conversation, the more Esme talked, the more she made sense in her own mind. The class was hanging on her every word, but Mrs Francis would not budge on the matter.

"Violence is always wrong, and two wrongs do not make a right, Esme. Now, I think that's all we have time for today."

As if on cue, the bell rang, signalling the end of first period. Esme gathered her notebook in her arms and moved towards the door, with Florian following closely behind.

"Your argument is convincing," he said firmly. "The Sparkmasters have been hurting dragons for years. It's about time someone stood up to them."

"They sound awful," said Esme. "Why are they called Sparkmasters?"

"Well, it all goes back to their beginnings," said Florian, keen to explain. "The Sparkmasters began their brutal campaign for power by using storm dragons exclusively. It was easy for them to bully the dragons into firing bolts of lightning directly onto the buildings of towns that they wanted to raid. No thatched roof was safe, and neither were those who dwelled underneath. The damage it caused was an immediate way for the Sparkmasters to intimidate."

"So they got their name by using storm dragons?"

"Exactly," said Florian. "Of course, we all know that each type of dragon is amazing in its own way. It didn't take the Sparkmasters long to realise that, and so, over time, although the history of their name goes back to their use of storm dragons, they have gone on to exploit the power of any other kind of dragon that they can. Earth dragons, water dragons, lava dragons, you name it! If there's a dragon the Sparkmasters can use, they won't hold back."

"I just can't imagine how anyone wouldn't want to help," Esme said. "Dragons are such wonderful creatures. I can't bear the thought of sitting back, knowing that someone out there is hurting them."

"Maybe you should do something, Esme," Florian

said. "You'll have your own dragon one day."

"Do you think my dragon would want to help?"

"I honestly don't know," Florian said doubtfully.

"When do we get our dragons?" Esme asked.

"It really depends on how fast you progress through your studies," he explained. "The academy will probably pair you up with a dragon after a couple of months. You'll be able to start training together then. That said, the pairing can come sooner or later, depending on your performance."

"Interesting…" Esme said thoughtfully.

"Esme!" Finn called from the other end of the corridor as she ran towards her. "How was your first class?"

"It was certainly different," Esme said. "Finn, have you met Florian?"

"I've seen him around," Finn said cheerily. "Nice to officially meet you, Florian!"

"Nice to meet you too, Finn," he replied.

"Come on, Esme," said Finn. "We need to get to

our second class. You're with me for periods two and three. It's lunch after that. Felix will probably need your help. We'll spend the rest of the break outside – it will be nice to get some fresh air. Some students just sleep or study during that time, but for those with a dragon, it's flight class. After that, there are two more periods before dinner. You're with me for those, so I'll make sure that you get to them all on time. You'll get the hang of the timetable soon enough!"

"Thanks, Finn," Esme said gratefully.

"You're welcome! Come on now, else we'll be late!"

Esme waved goodbye to Florian as she was rushed off to her next class.

Chapter Ten

Each remaining period of the day went by much too quickly for Esme. Her head felt foggy by the end of it. There had been so much to take in. Although she had made notes, she wished the classes were longer so she could really absorb all the information.

There was so much more to dragons than she had imagined. They had been studied and documented for thousands of years. Esme was learning all about their eating habits, migration patterns, and their whole way of life. It was like being transported into a whole other world.

"How is your first day going?" Felix asked as he cleared the kitchen in preparation for dinner.

Esme responded by slumping onto a wooden chair. She sighed heavily.

"That bad, huh?" he asked sympathetically.

"I'm happy to be here. There's just so much to take in!" Esme said sadly. "I feel like all the others have been here so much longer than me. I've got so much catching up to do."

"First days are always overwhelming. You'll quickly get the hang of everything," Felix said reassuringly. "Besides, a lot of the others are just as clueless as you, so don't worry. Everyone around here is supportive. If you need a little help, don't hesitate to ask."

"I'm sure you're right," Esme replied. "It has been a busy day."

"Let's get to work on making dinner. This evening's meal is grilled cheese sandwiches and tomato soup. The soup's already done, so you can start serving it up. I'll keep an eye on the sandwiches."

"Thanks, Felix," said Esme, getting up and beginning to ladle the soup into bowls.

"Happy to help. While we're working, you could talk me through what you're learning. It might help to break things down a little."

"Mrs Francis talked about Sparkmasters," Esme said seriously.

"Ah, yes," Felix said regretfully. "All those poor dragons. I can't imagine."

"Why hasn't anything been done to stop them?" Esme asked desperately. "Surely someone must have tried to do something?"

"Oh, many have tried. But none have succeeded," Felix explained. "Sparkmasters have a way of breaking down the minds of dragons. Dragons who are used to humans are particularly susceptible to it. Many dragons, and even some humans, have lost their lives to this."

Deep in thought, Esme listened to the hissing of the sandwiches in the frying pans.

"Something has to be done," she whispered, more to herself than to Felix.

"There's not much we can do," he said.

"Is there a way to protect dragons from being influenced by Sparkmasters?" she asked.

"If there is, no one has found it yet," Felix replied. "There are many lone dragons out in the wild. They can be so vulnerable to humans with bad intentions."

"I hate the thought of a dragon being manipulated into a life of misery."

"Absolutely. You know how long dragons live. Years feel like days to them, and the length of a human life is merely a drop in the ocean. Let's not get too down about it though. Are you done with that soup?"

"Yes."

"Excellent. If you could scoop these sandwiches onto plates, that would be great."

"No problem," said Esme, moving over to the opposite side of the kitchen.

"If you put your mind to it, Esme, I'm sure you could come up with a way to help defeat the Sparkmasters."

Chapter Eleven

As the weeks went by, when she wasn't in class or helping in the kitchen, Esme poured herself into her studies. Occasionally, Finn would tell her to take a break, but even when they went for a walk into town together, Esme would look over her notes as soon as they sat down.

Esme was used to working hard. To her, studying was fun. She enjoyed being quizzed by Felix as she washed dishes or stirred the soup. She loved it when her teachers pushed her to do better, and when they helped her to succeed. In turn, the teachers loved Esme because she was a fast learner, often asking intelligent questions. The other students loved her because her enthusiasm was contagious. And of course, Felix loved her because she was good company for him in the kitchen.

For the first time in her life, Esme was working hard at something that she genuinely believed in.

For the first time in her life, she was *happy*. There was only one thing missing – just that one thing that would make Esme's life perfect.

Her own dragon.

As her time at Dragon Academy turned from weeks to months, more and more of Esme's classmates were matched with a dragon. Finn offered to take her to watch the ceremonies, but Esme always refused. As much as she wanted to see the dragons, and to be close enough to see their scales move as they breathed, she held back.

It's not your turn yet.

Esme didn't hesitate to remind herself that she would have to work for it. She wanted to prove to herself that she could do it. She needed to be able to show her dragon that she was worthy of them. She knew that upon meeting her very own dragon for the first time, it would be hers for life. That moment would be everything. She wanted it to be special.

When Finn and some of the other students would go out near the cliffs, or to the stables to hang out, Esme would stay in her room. Sometimes, when she looked wistfully out of the window, she could see dragons flying in the distance. It filled her with determination, inspiring her to work even harder in her classes.

***

"Good morning, Felix," Esme said as she walked into the kitchen.

She took her apron down from a peg on the wall. Felix had embroidered her name on it after her first month at the academy.

"Good morning, Esme," he said. "Did you sleep well?"

"Not really," she admitted. "I spent most of the night studying for that dragon biology test. It's tomorrow."

Felix clicked his tongue, making a sound of disapproval.

"You know you need to sleep more," he said. "You don't let yourself get enough rest. You hardly ever relax."

"I come and hang out with you all the time," Esme said innocently.

"Why don't you take some time off to hang out

with Finn and her friends? Go into town for a while. Go shopping or something."

"It's a nice idea," Esme replied. "It just wouldn't feel right though. There's way too much to do around here."

"Well, at least go for a bit of a walk outside, just to get some fresh air, and to clear your head."

"Perhaps," Esme said, a little dismissively.

"I give up," Felix said, defeated but concerned. "I'm only looking out for your health, Esme."

"I know you are," Esme said with a smile. "Thank you. I promise I'm ok though. I'm fascinated by everything I'm learning, and I love working with you. I'm not stressed at all. I *promise*. In fact, this is the happiest I've ever been."

Looking into Esme's eyes, Felix could see that she was sincere.

"I'm glad," he said with a serious nod. "Now, do me a favour and mix up this salad. Headmaster Osgood has been on my back recently for not serving enough vegetables. I'll show him vegetables!"

As Felix began chopping the carrots with force, Esme smiled and, shaking her head, walked over to help with the salad.

"Have you heard anything about when I might be getting my dragon?" she asked. "Have you heard anything about it at a teachers' meeting? You go to those, right?"

"There's been talk of it," he confirmed. "You know I avoid those meetings wherever possible. They're always painfully boring. Some of the teachers do stop by to keep me updated though. Everyone is happy with your progress so far."

"Does that mean I'll get my dragon soon?"

"I don't know when exactly you will get your dragon, Esme. I'm sure you're on the right path. You've just got to stick with it. You will be assigned a dragon when your teachers – and Headmaster Osgood – agree that you're ready."

"Then how can I become ready?" Esme asked insistently.

"I honestly don't know," said Felix. "You would have to ask your teachers."

"Fine," Esme said firmly as the first of the students began to show up for lunch. "I will."

Chapter Twelve

Esme asked her teachers, but all of them gave the same response, advising her to keep working hard and be patient.

Their answer wasn't good enough for Esme. Frustrated, that evening, she paced around her room. The beauty of the glowing orange sunset shining through the window did nothing to soothe her thoughts.

"I don't see why you're so upset about this," Finn said, trying to be sympathetic.

Esme desperately wanted to put her emotions into words that her friend could understand. She took a deep breath to calm herself, and then tried to explain.

"I've given up so much to be here. At first, it was just to learn about dragons. But then, when I realised the academy could offer me more – my own dragon – I haven't been able to think about much else since! I work hard every day, and often well into the night. I'm doing everything that is asked of me, and sometimes it feels like there's nothing more I can do. I wish someone would just tell me exactly what it is I need to do to get my own dragon!"

Exasperated, Esme forcefully sat down on the edge of her bed.

"Nobody is asking you to work without a break, Esme. I know that being here means a lot to you. You'll just have to trust the process," Finn said gently. "The teachers have been doing this for a long time, and they know a lot more than we do. When you're ready to be paired with a dragon, they will know. That's what my father says, anyway."

A thought exploded like a firework in Esme's mind.

"That's it!" she said, clicking her fingers as she accepted her idea. "Your father! If anyone knows how I can be ready enough for a dragon, it will be him. He is the headmaster, after all! He must know!"

"Right, so just relax and trust that…"

"Thanks, Finn!" Esme said, no longer listening as she rushed out of the room.

She slammed the door behind her, leaving a confused Finn to shrug and go back to reading her magazine.

Esme rushed down flight after flight of stairs, nearly bumping into a group of students along the way. They glared at her as she mumbled a quick apology before running off again.

Finally, she turned a corner and stopped in front of the closed door of the headmaster's office. Taking a moment to control her breathing, which had turned into wild panting from running down the many flights of stairs, she straightened her uniform and knocked on the door.

"Come in," came a voice from inside the office.

Esme opened the door, slipped in, and closed it behind her.

"Hello, Esme," said Headmaster Osgood. "Please, sit down."

As she took a seat, Esme noticed that Headmaster Osgood looked shaken, as if something terrible had just happened.

"Sir, what's wrong?" she asked.

He sighed deeply, sinking low in his chair as he gestured to a piece of paper on his desk.

"I've just received this letter from a former student," he said quietly. "She lives in a town not too far from here. Wishing to teach others, she moved back there with her dragon after graduation."

"That sounds amazing," Esme said cautiously, realising that there must be more to the story.

"The Sparkmasters destroyed her whole town. She tried to protect it – and its people – but they were outnumbered. Her dragon died trying to protect her."

Unable to keep his composure, Headmaster Osgood put his head in his hands. Esme sat back in her seat, totally shocked.

"The Sparkmasters have attacked some of the other towns nearby," Headmaster Osgood said after a moment of tense silence. "By targeting places that aren't too far from Dragon Academy, they know it serves to taunt us. They're rubbing their victories in our faces."

"*Why* can't we fight back?" Esme asked, full of emotion.

"That's not the way we do things," he said.

Esme could see the doubt in his eyes.

"What if they were to attack the academy?" she insisted. "Surely you would want to defend it?"

"They won't attack us," he said. "They threatened it generations ago, but there is something about this place – something that none of us fully understand. It protects us. That's why dragons come here. That's why people who feel drawn to dragons come here."

"Do you think it was wrong of your friend to try defending her town?" Esme asked.

"No, of course not," Headmaster Osgood said sharply. "It was self-defence. Sending an army of dragon riders from this academy to battle the Sparkmasters would not be self-defence. It would be against everything we stand for."

"What if every town had enough dragon riders living there to protect everyone?"

"Where are you going with this?" he asked, raising

an eyebrow suspiciously.

"Assign your dragon riders to live in towns nearby," Esme said. "Call it an exchange programme, or a field trip or something. Then, in the event of an attack from the Sparkmasters, we would be ready."

Headmaster Osgood stared at Esme as he considered her suggestion. Finally, he shook his head.

"It wouldn't be possible. Our job is to educate students about dragons. When we pair a student with a dragon, it is done with peace and harmony in mind. It's not our job to fight a war with the Sparkmasters."

"But people are dying!" Esme exclaimed. "Dragons are dying! You said so yourself! I thought the purpose of Dragon Academy was to protect dragons!"

"Maybe it's not our job to help in this case, Esme," Headmaster Osgood said sternly.

"You have the power to stop this," she said, respectfully trying hard not to raise her voice. "You have the power to free those dragons who are being exploited by the Sparkmasters. You have the power to stop the Sparkmasters from raiding towns and killing people. You *have* that power, and yet here you are doing nothing. That's what you're telling me: you're *choosing* to do nothing."

"I can't…"

"What if it was my village?" she demanded, furiously cutting him off. "What if it was my family on the line? Would you do something then? If it was a town full of innocent people with families? With children? Tell me! Would you do something then?"

Headmaster Osgood didn't respond, but Esme could see the answer in his eyes.

She turned and strode angrily towards the door. Just as she was about to leave the room, he spoke.

"You will be assigned your dragon next week, Esme. The rest will be up to you then."

Chapter Thirteen

After the heated discussion she'd had with Headmaster Osgood, Esme stumbled into bed in a daze. She didn't hear a word when Finn tried to talk to her. Once Finn had fallen asleep, Esme's mind continued to whirl.

In a week, she would have her dragon. In just seven more days, all of her struggles and sacrifices would amount to something incredible.

Esme thought about the same thing over and over again as the days went by in a blur.

In seven days, this will all be worth it, she thought as she took a dragon history test.

In six days, I will meet my lifelong partner, my friend from another species, she reminded herself as she helped Felix slice apples.

In five days…

"Esme? Are you listening?" Mrs Francis asked.

"Yes Miss," Esme said quickly. "You were talking about the thickness of different dragon scales."

"That's right," the teacher said with a nod. "Thank you for paying attention! Everyone should be. Some of you are getting your dragons very soon, after all."

"I can't wait," Florian whispered to Esme as Mrs Francis turned around to write on the board.

"Same here," Esme replied with a huge smile.

Her smile faded as she turned back to the notebook in front of her. Florian couldn't help but notice.

"Are you ok?" he asked.

Esme glanced up at Florian's worried expression.

"What if my dragon doesn't like me?" she asked, chewing on the top of her pen.

"It's going to love you," he said reassuringly. "Everyone does!"

"But dragons are different," Esme replied. "They see more than people can. They have other senses, and can pick up on a lot more than we do. What if it doesn't like what it sees in me?"

"If it doesn't fall completely in love with you the moment it sees you, and if it isn't loyal to you for the rest of its life, it's missing out, Esme," Florian said kindly. "You're the most loyal, hardworking, dedicated, and kind person I know. Any dragon would be lucky to have you as its human."

"Thank you, Florian," Esme mumbled, blushing at his praise.

Florian gave Esme's shoulder a friendly squeeze before turning back to his work. She smiled to herself as she doodled little drawings of dragons in the margins of her notebook.

I wonder what kind of dragon I'll be paired with. Maybe a water dragon! I'll ride the waves with it. I'll have to learn how to swim if that's the case. Maybe it would teach me. Or perhaps I'll get an earth dragon. That would be nice.

Esme drew a picture of herself standing with a dragon deep within the forest. She thought back to the days when she'd walk along the path near her village.

On those walks, I used to daydream about

everything that I wanted my life to be. And now, I'm so much closer to getting everything I've ever wanted. Would my family be proud?

As Esme's mind turned to thoughts of her parents, she could feel a longing in her heart. Would her father be proud of her hard work? Would her mother be happy that she was finally content? Would it be enough for them that she was safe, loved, and pleased to be on a path of her own choosing?

Unusually for Esme, her mind then completely drifted from the rest of the lecture. Instead, she turned a page in her notebook to write a letter:

Dear Mother and Father,

I made it to Dragon Academy. I've made a wonderful new friend here. I met her on my journey into Harauin and she kindly helped me with the admissions process.

I work in the kitchen to pay my way. The cook is an amazing gentleman named Felix. He's close to Father's age, and very kind. I enjoy working with him.

I'm doing well in my classes, and I study whenever I can. Many of my teachers have said that I'm one of the most diligent students they've taught.

In a few days' time, I'm going to be assigned my very own dragon. Then, I'll have more classes with that dragon. I look forward to learning even more. One day, when I graduate, my dragon and I will be free to travel the world together. I have a couple of plans for that point, but there's still plenty for me to do in the meantime.

At this point, I'd like to ask you both: may I please come and visit?

Esme sat and stared at the last line of the letter. She then scratched it out, not sure of how best to ask her parents if she was still welcome back home. She rewrote the question over and over – until she had crossed out her attempts so many times that there was a hole in the paper. She wanted to know that her parents were ok, and that the farm was doing well. She just wanted to see them – whether for a cup of tea, or to go and help with the harvest. She wanted them to know that she was happy and well.

Her eyes misty with tears, she ripped the messy sheet of paper out of her notebook, crumpled it up, and wrote a new letter:

Dear Mother and Father,

I am safe and happy. I hope you are both doing well. I miss you.

Love,

Esme.

That was the letter that Esme posted from the academy. And that was the letter that arrived at the small farm in a small village.

That was the letter that Esme's mother kept to herself, reading it night after night, with tears pouring down her face.

Chapter Fourteen

our days before she could be assigned a dragon, along with several other students, Esme was required to take a written test.

"How should we study for it?" she asked in class.

"You don't," Mrs Francis explained. "The purpose of the test is to assess your personality. That way, we can get a better idea of which dragons you could potentially be paired with. For example, students with a more relaxed approach would be a good match to balance out a dragon that's wilder and more energetic."

Finn and Esme talked amongst themselves as they walked to the exam room.

"I wonder what kind of questions it will ask," said Finn.

"Have you heard about this test before?" Esme asked.

"I've heard other students mention it, but I've never paid much attention," Finn admitted. "Mind you, if it's a personality test, I doubt there can be such a thing as a wrong answer."

"I suppose we'll find out," Esme said.

As they entered the exam room, Finn and Esme took a seat at their assigned desks near the back. Florian walked in, nodded to them, and sat close by.

"Florian," Esme whispered. "Do you know anything about this test?"

He shrugged his shoulders, and spoke quietly.

"There are no grades on a test like this," he explained. "There are no right or wrong answers. Just relax and answer honestly."

Soon enough, the exam invigilator handed every student in the room a sheet of paper containing a list of questions, and a pencil with which to answer.

Taking a deep breath, Esme set to work.

Question one: am I a sociable person? I'm not sure what to write for that. Hmm...

Trying not to give it too much thought, she eventually wrote her answer:

Not particularly, but I like being sociable when I feel up to it.

The rest of the questions were just as confusing. Amongst them, was much ambiguity, such as: "Do you have a good work/life balance?", "Do you find yourself struggling to talk to new people?" and "Would you consider yourself a happy person?".

As she went through each of the questions, they gave Esme cause to reflect on her life. It made her smile to remember how far she'd come in the last few months, but it also made her sad to think about everything she'd left behind.

The next question – "Do you have any regrets?" – sent her mind whirling.

She wanted to say that she regretted nothing. But she couldn't. She regretted her mother's tears and her father's anger, and the look in their eyes when she told them she was leaving and that nothing could change her mind. Although everything after that moment had been wonderful, and Esme was happy, it didn't serve to erase her regrets. And so, scrawling on the paper and smudging the pencil marks a little, she answered the question honestly.

The next question – "When was the last time you were truly angry?" – was an easy one for Esme to answer. She didn't hesitate on it for even a moment. The conversation she'd had with Headmaster Osgood in his office had made her blood boil. What she wrote on the paper made her feelings abundantly clear:

Headmaster Osgood understands the pain of the woman who lost her dragon to the Sparkmasters, and yet he says we are best off doing nothing about it. I just can't understand it! I wish I could, because I hold him, and of course, Dragon Academy in high regard. It hurts me to think that there's nothing we can do to help other dragons from falling victim to the Sparkmasters.

The final question – "Why do you want a dragon?" – made Esme sit back and think. The big clock above the invigilator's desk was ticking away the minutes, and the room echoed with the sound of pencils scratching against paper. Esme keenly reminded herself that she needed to make her answer a good one.

Before she'd had the heated conversation in Headmaster Osgood's office, her explanation as to why she wanted a dragon would have been centred on the fact that she had always felt like a part of her was missing, and that she needed a dragon to resolve that. Having had the conversation in the headmaster's office though, Esme's thoughts on why she wanted a dragon had changed. And so, she reflected upon that in her answer:

I want to go on a journey with my dragon. I want us to work together, to protect other dragons and innocent people. I want an ally who will have my back in the battles we may face. With a foundation of unconditional love and friendship, I want my dragon and I to make it our life's mission to fight for the greater good.

For a good few minutes, Esme stared at the last sentence of her answer. She felt as though there was more to be said, but in the moment, and against the clock, it was the best she had to offer. The questions had been emotionally demanding and she had given them her all under test conditions.

I'm almost afraid that I won't get a dragon at all. What if they see my answers as problematic and refuse to match me with one? After all, Dragon Academy has a responsibility to their dragons first and foremost. Oh well, I've done all I can. I've been honest. I would never want to be given a dragon under any false pretences.

Making sure that she had signed her name on the

paper, Esme stood up and took it to the invigilator at the front of the exam room, surprised to discover that all the other students were still working on their tests.

"Thank you, Esme," the invigilator said quietly as he took her paper.

"Thank you, Sir," she replied in a whisper as she turned to leave the room.

Chapter Fifteen

After the test, Esme didn't talk very much. She ate, slept, studied, and went to classes on autopilot. She was nervous, excited, and highly aware of the importance of what was about to take place.

As three days turned to two, and then two to one, the tension grew. With just one night to go before being assigned her dragon, Esme couldn't sleep. She tossed and turned in her bed, staring up at the ceiling, then staring out of the window, then staring at the wall. Finally, she couldn't take it anymore. She got up, put on her slippers and nightgown, and opened the door. Finn, who was snoring at full volume, did not even notice when she left.

Esme walked down the stairs as quietly as she could. She wasn't heading for anywhere in particular. Finally, she ended up at the door to the kitchen. Knowing where the key was, she unlocked it and let herself in.

After closing the door behind her and walking further towards the pantry, she froze as she saw about eight other students already there. Noticing that they had been spotted, the students froze too, crumbs on their faces and horror in their eyes.

"How did you get in here?" Esme asked.

One of the students pointed at the window through which during mealtimes, they were able to get food from the kitchen to take into the dining area.

"I thought that was locked," Esme said, crossing her arms over her chest.

"The lock is old," said a familiar voice.

It was Florian. He stepped out into the light and smiled at Esme, biscuit crumbs all over his chin.

"It's pretty easy to pick it," he said with a cheery grin.

"I hope none of you take too much while you're here," Esme said. "I'll be the prime suspect if you do!"

"Hey, there's nothing to worry about," said one of the other students.

Esme recognised her from a couple of classes. Her name was Vivian.

"We only come here on special occasions, or for emergencies," Vivian explained. "We never eat enough for Felix to notice that it's gone."

"Fair enough," Esme said, nodding her head in agreement. "So, what is tonight? A special occasion or an emergency?"

"Maybe it's a bit of both," said Florian. "Would you like a pastry? We found them at the back of the pantry. They're a little stale, but still pretty good for a late-night snack."

"Those are the pastries that Felix keeps for feeding the birds," said Esme. "I've snacked on them myself many times. Pass one over."

She sat on one of the countertops and enjoyed her late-night snack, listening to the other students talk about their worries for the big day, for they too, were due to be assigned a dragon.

"What if my dragon doesn't like me?" one of them announced sadly.

"What if they like you at first, and then years later, they don't?" Vivian added. "Once you've grown attached to them, what if they get to know you better, only to find that they don't like you then?"

"What if I'm not good enough for my dragon?" another student mumbled. "What if it sees something in me that I don't see in myself? What if it knows I'm not good enough just by looking at me?"

Esme began to grow tired as she listened to all of her fellow students' deepest fears. Finally, she slid off the counter.

"I think we should all have more faith in ourselves, and in our dragons," she said.

She could see that her words hadn't helped. She hadn't really expected them to. She had the same fears.

"Don't forget to lock the window when you leave," Esme said, turning to leave the kitchen and go back to her room.

Florian followed her outside into the hallway.

"They're just scared, Esme," he said. "You can't blame them for that."

"I'm scared too," she protested.

"Come on," said Florian. "Let's go for a walk to clear our heads."

"Ok," said Esme. "I won't be able to get to sleep now anyway."

Silent apart from their footsteps, the pair walked the hallways of the academy. Eventually, they found themselves close to the headmaster's office.

Florian suddenly held up his hand, motioning to Esme to keep quiet and still.

"Do you hear that?" he whispered cautiously.

Esme listened carefully. As the two of them edged closer towards the door of Headmaster Osgood's office, they could overhear a heated discussion.

"I think our best option is to give her a choice," said an unfamiliar voice from behind the door.

"We've never done that before," Headmaster Osgood responded to the person unknown to Esme and Florian. "*We've* always assigned the students their dragons. That's how we've always done things!"

"Things need to change," the unfamiliar voice said. "Don't you see that? Nothing will get any better unless something changes. I've read the answers on that girl's test paper several times. I've seen the fire in her eyes. Don't be so set in your ways. Nobody else has the vision to assign her a dragon. She needs to choose the dragon. The dragon needs to choose her."

"My council and I have successfully paired hundreds of students and dragons," Headmaster Osgood protested. "Nothing needs to change!"

"That's easy for you to say. You are safe within these walls. That girl is ready to think beyond the academy; she's ready to put herself in danger for the greater good."

Upon hearing a pause in the conversation behind the door of the office, Esme looked questioningly at Florian, not quite sure what to make of what they were witnessing. Quickly noticing the outside door handle move downwards, they ducked down behind a large wooden banister.

"Let the girl choose," the unfamiliar figure called back firmly into the office as he stepped out into the hallway alone.

Esme and Florian exchanged glances, and then quickly walked up the stairs.

"What was that about?" she finally whispered when they were two flights up.

"I don't know," Florian said quietly. "But it must have something to do with the dragon assignment tomorrow. I guess we'll have to wait and find out."

The pair bid each other goodnight. When Esme got back to her bedroom, Finn was still fast asleep. Slipping back into bed unnoticed, Esme gazed up at the ceiling, unable to forget what she had heard.

She needs to choose the dragon. The dragon needs to choose her…

The words echoed in Esme's mind until she fell asleep.

Chapter Sixteen

By morning, Esme was a chaotic bundle of energy and nerves. She served breakfast, but her mind wasn't on the task. When Felix tried to talk to her, she gave him only the shortest of responses. He smiled, not wishing to press her. Instead, he made her a hearty breakfast of pancakes, bacon, and cinnamon apples. It was, after all, a special day.

After breakfast, instead of going to their regular classes, Esme and a small group of students were invited to head to the stables.

"Now, all the dragons that you're about to meet today are very young," Mrs Fringle explained sternly as she guided the group along a dusty path. "Once they have been with their assigned human for a few months, a dragon will grow quickly. They may seem like puppies now, but as you have covered in your studies so far, you must never underestimate any dragon."

"Are you nervous?" Finn whispered to Esme as they walked.

Esme could only nod, the lump in her throat preventing her from speaking.

The group stopped at the doors to the stable.

"Single file line, please," ordered Mrs Fringle.

Everyone lined up silently. Esme found herself at the very back of the queue. She watched her fellow students go one by one into the stable, each of them emotionally coming back out with their dragons.

Some students carried their dragon in their arms, holding them like babies. Other dragons bounded excitedly along at the feet of their equally excited owners. There were so many kinds of dragons coming out from the stable: storm dragons, earth dragons, water dragons, cloud dragons, and even a star dragon!

I wonder what kind of dragon I will be assigned.

All of the students and the dragons looked so happy. As Esme watched the assigned students walk back towards the academy with their dragons, she took a step closer to the stable.

Next, it was Finn's turn to go into the stable to collect her dragon. She gave Esme a sheepish thumbs-up signal before walking inside. After a couple of minutes, she emerged with a dragon. Her face was glowing, and she wore the biggest smile that Esme had ever seen. Upon closer inspection, Esme could see that curled up and sleeping in Finn's arms, was a water dragon.

"Good luck!" Finn enthused as she walked away from Esme, and back towards the academy.

Florian was next to enter the stable. He came out with a dark red dragon clinging to his back. Esme wasn't sure what kind of dragon it was, but when Florian noticed her staring, he called across to her.

"It's a rock dragon!" he shouted.

He nodded at Esme as he set off on his way back to the academy. Esme smiled, happy for her friend.

Her happiness was soon swallowed by the anticipation of the moment.

"Esme?" asserted Mrs Fringle, motioning for her to move forward.

Esme took a deep breath and stepped into the stable, immediately noticing the overpowering scent of fresh straw. Light shone through the small cracks in the roof, illuminating dust particles that sailed through the air.

As she walked further into the large stable, the loose straw and dirt on the ground crunching beneath her feet, she looked up to see Headmaster Osgood stood there.

"This way," he said.

Esme followed him to the back of the stable. When she peered around the corner, she could see three little dragons. One was dark purple, with blue streaks like rivers running down its back. It sat in the corner and stared at her intensely. Esme recognised it as a water dragon.

The second dragon was a deep blue, with golden wings and horns. It was curled up sleeping on the floor. As it breathed, its horns flickered with lightning. Esme recognised that type of dragon too.

A storm dragon.

The last dragon to catch her eye had been sleeping next to the storm dragon until Esme had moved closer. It was slightly more muscular than the other two dragons, and would surely grow to be powerful. A lava dragon, it was scarlet red with fiery eyes and a happy grin. It playfully jumped up and flapped the straw from its wings. Esme was delighted to see that on the underside of its wings was a majestic deep green. The dragon looked at her for a moment, then cautiously took a couple of steps forward.

Esme crouched down and held out her hand for the dragon. It sniffed it, still wary of her, and then, as though it had made up its mind, put its chin in her palm. Esme smiled and stroked the smooth, warm scales of the dragon as gently as she could. The dragon raised its tail in contentment. Esme noticed the tiny flame at the end of it, remembering from her studies that it must stay alight and never go out.

"I bet you have to be careful with that," she said to the dragon. "Especially with all of this hay around."

"Any lava dragon in a stable certainly has to be careful," said Headmaster Osgood.

Esme jumped, having forgotten that the headmaster was there. The dragon felt her surprise and pulled away, hurrying back to play with the storm dragon who had just sweetly chirped. The two young dragons batted and growled playfully at each other.

"Which one is mine?" Esme asked.

"It's up to you," said Headmaster Osgood. "The choice is yours."

The conversation I overheard last night... They must have been talking about me!

Esme tried to seem surprised. She didn't want the headmaster to know that she'd eavesdropped.

"I thought it was your job to choose a dragon for me," she said.

"Pick one," the headmaster insisted.

Esme turned back to the three dragons. When she took a step forward, the lava dragon looked up at her. She crouched down and held out her hand again. The lava dragon smiled widely and scurried over, jumping up to put its front claws on her knees.

"Hello," Esme whispered, stroking behind the lava dragon's tiny ears.

"I think your dragon has chosen you," Headmaster Osgood said proudly.

Excited by everything that was going on around him, the little dragon sneezed and fell backwards, landing rather clumsily. Instinctively, Esme placed a hand on his back, wanting to make sure that he was ok. The dragon chirped happily, signalling that he was unharmed.

With her hand away from the dragon, Esme could feel a slight burning sensation running through her fingers and her palm.

That must be the connection that was mentioned in dragon empathy class. Wow! I didn't expect to feel it so soon! This is incredible!

"Come with me," Esme said to the lava dragon, sure of their rapport.

The dragon blinked at her, and then jumped up, putting its claws on her shoulders, and licking her cheek. Esme giggled and scooped the dragon up into her arms.

"This is the one," she said.

"Excellent," said Headmaster Osgood. "Go back to the fourth room on the second floor for dragon induction. Congratulations, Esme."

"Thank you, Sir."

Esme walked happily out of the stable with the little dragon snuggled close to her. She could feel its tiny heart beating. Just as she had been hoping for, she finally felt complete.

"I think I'm going to call you Freedom," she whispered to the dragon.

The dragon chirped in response.

"Ok. Freedom it is," Esme said, grinning from ear to ear.

Chapter Seventeen

For each student who had been assigned a dragon on that vital day, the next two months were all about bonding. The dragons slept in the bedrooms with their respective humans. The humans fed them, played with them, and brought them everywhere. When the two months were up, the dragons had grown to almost the size of a horse. With them being too big to stay in the bedrooms with the students, they had to sleep in the stables. It was hard for everyone who had grown used to the comfort of always having their dragon with them.

As they settled their dragons down in the stables for their first night of sleep there, Esme, Finn and Florian took their time. They were in no rush to head back inside.

"Hurricane is incredibly strong," Finn said proudly. "I'm sure she could control the whole ocean if she wanted to. Water dragons are so powerful."

"All types of dragon are powerful in their own way," said Florian.

He tenderly stroked the snout of his rock dragon, Terra.

"I bet mine is more powerful than yours though," Finn retorted.

"Maybe, maybe not," said Florian. "It's not all about being the most powerful. It's about the bond between a human and their dragon."

Finn shrugged.

Whilst stroking Freedom's snout, Esme calmly watched the exchange between her friends. Freedom wasn't the biggest dragon, nor was he the most powerful. If he was above average in anything, it was in his playfulness and mischievous behaviour. Esme didn't mind. In fact, she loved that about him.

Suddenly, the peacefulness of the night was interrupted as Vivian charged into the stable, bursting the doors open in a frantic state of panic.

"The Sparkmasters are flying over!" she shouted.

Esme exchanged glances with everyone around

her. They all hurried outside and, looking up into the night, they could see outlines of dragons and glimmers of lantern light in the sky above them.

"Where are they going?" Florian asked, his voice low and afraid.

Vivian pointed up at the sky, tracing her finger along the route of the Sparkmasters overhead.

"The nearest village in that direction is about a day's walk from here," she announced.

"They're heading in the direction of *my* village!" Esme exclaimed.

Horrified, she ran back into the stable and called out for Freedom. Although still in training and not always the best at recall, the young dragon jumped to attention, sensing the urgency in Esme's voice.

Apart from a few short test flights around the academy during lessons, Esme hadn't been on Freedom's back for any serious amount of time.

"I'm not sure that we're ready for this, Freedom," Esme said truthfully. "But the Sparkmasters are heading towards my village. My family are there. I must protect them. Are you with me?"

Freedom let out a low growl, and Esme could feel the familiar burning sensation in the palm of her hand.

"Thank you," she whispered to Freedom as she pulled herself onto the dragon's back.

"Esme!" Finn shouted. "What are you doing?"

Esme didn't have time to think or explain. She just had to trust herself, and her dragon.

"I'm going to do what's right," she called back.

With the ember at the end of his tail burning brightly, Freedom ran out of the stable and towards a take-off point near the edge of the cliff. Once there, he bounced up into the air, spreading his wings for flight.

Chapter Eighteen

Esme didn't need to follow the path of the Sparkmasters. She knew the way to her village, and was determined to get there first. Although it was dangerous to do so – especially at night – she flew as close to the ground as she could. She couldn't risk being seen by the Sparkmasters.

Luckily, Freedom knew what he was doing. Esme trusted her dragon and was able to confidently whisper directions into his ear.

"There, left there. See that road? Follow it!"

What had been a day's walk for Esme was a fifteen-minute flight for Freedom. Together, they could soon see the lights of her village.

"Land in the centre," Esme told Freedom, almost instinctively.

As Freedom's feet touched upon the cobblestones, a woman walking nearby screamed in horror. Esme ignored her and instead, ran towards the village bell. Pulling the cord as hard as she could, the noise echoed through the streets, warning everyone of danger. As doors began to open, Esme jumped upon Freedom's back.

"Enemies are coming!" she announced to the emerging crowd. "I'm here to help. Don't attack us! Attack them! Spread the word, and quickly!"

Esme could only hope that her explanation would be enough, because that's all she could offer. The next second, the first explosion hit.

"Come on, Freedom," Esme yelled.

Freedom jumped into the air, nearly knocking into a Sparkmaster's dragon. The dragon opened its mouth to shoot fire at Freedom, but Freedom was faster, burning the Sparkmaster off the back of the dragon. With its master gone, the dragon looked confused. Freedom hissed, communicating with it. It looked up at Esme.

"Leave, or help us," Esme said. "Your choice."

The dragon responded by flying up higher into the air to push a Sparkmaster off from another dragon's back.

Esme smiled.

"Watch out, Freedom!" she called out suddenly.

Freedom baulked to avoid the fire being shot at them from another dragon.

"Are you ok?" Esme shouted.

Freedom grunted reassuringly and lunged at another rider. The rider, realising what was happening, jumped onto Freedom's back to try and attack Esme. Freedom rolled upside-down, and the rider fell down to the street below to be captured by the villagers, who still appeared to be more confused than focused overall.

"Go there!" Esme commanded as she pointed downwards.

Freedom dropped like a hawk onto an unsuspecting rider, pushing him off and freeing another dragon.

As she looked around on high-alert, Esme could see that Freedom had just unseated the last rider. There were no more Sparkmasters to be seen. Other dragons had been saved by fellow freed dragons, who were gathered above the village cobblestones to celebrate their victory.

"Freedom, tell these dragons about the academy," Esme instructed. "Tell them to go there. They'll be safe there."

Freedom called to the other dragons with a roar, and they seemed to understand. They flew off in the direction of the academy, leaving Freedom and Esme alone in the air.

Esme looked down at the villagers, many of whom still held weapons in their hands. Despite having already extinguished the few fires that the Sparkmasters had started, everyone was clearly still on edge.

"Don't hurt us!" Esme yelled in warning as Freedom came in to land.

Looking around in awe, the villagers backed away to make room.

"You don't have to be afraid of dragons anymore," Esme shouted. "Dragons only do bad things when they are under the command of bad people. At the heart of it, there is no such thing as a bad dragon."

"Esme?" a familiar voice called out from the crowd.

Esme looked around, finally meeting the

concerned gaze of her father. Her mother was stood there beside him.

"Hello, Father. Hello, Mother," she said. "I've missed you both so much."

"We've missed you too, Esme," said Amethyst, tears glistening in her eyes.

"You're riding a dragon," Declan said gruffly.

Esme nodded.

"I tried to tell you," she said. "They're not what you think they are."

"But they attacked us," her mother protested.

"They were being controlled by Sparkmasters," Esme explained firmly. "Dragons are not the enemy."

"Hmm…" her father mused.

Amethyst turned her attention towards Freedom. The dragon noticed, and humbly took a few slow steps forward.

"You can pet him if you'd like to, Mother," Esme said.

"Amethyst, don't," Declan warned.

Esme's mother didn't listen. Instead, she reached her hand out and stroked Freedom's snout. Freedom purred quietly.

"He's amazing, Esme," Amethyst whispered, comforted and enchanted by the dragon's sweet nature.

"He is," said Esme. "There's a whole world of dragons out there, Mother – as kind and as gentle as Freedom. I wish that you – and anyone else who doubts that – could see dragons for what they truly are."

Esme's mother took a step back before exchanging a thoughtful glance with her husband, who nodded back at her in agreement.

"You should go and help more dragons, Esme," said Amethyst. "You only want to do what's right by them, and by us. We can see that now."

"Thank you," said Esme. "You haven't seen the last of us. We'll be back."

"Be careful out there," said Amethyst. "Please."

The villagers began to move closer towards

Freedom. They still carried their weapons, but didn't seem intent on using them. Instead, they were amazed and curious. Knowing that it would take a long time for everyone to fully understand and trust dragons though, Esme wasn't willing to hang around and risk the safety of her friend.

"Let's go, Freedom," she said.

Still charged from the adrenaline of everything that had just happened, Freedom once again jumped up into the sky. He circled around the village for a while, allowing Esme to look down upon her old home.

"Freedom," she said. "What are your thoughts on doing that again? There are more villages to be saved, and more Sparkmasters out there to be defeated. Not only that, but if we work hard to teach more people about dragons, then maybe, just maybe, it will be for the good of people and dragons alike."

Freedom snorted happily in agreement, then roared into the night with a noise that made the very stars shake.

"Perfect," said Esme.

And it was.

Epilogue

It angered Headmaster Osgood to hear of what had happened in Esme's village. Although she had spoken with him at great length about taking on the Sparkmasters, there had always been a part of him that believed she wouldn't. Upon her return to Dragon Academy, Esme spent the next three days in her room, with Finn, Florian and Felix dropping by to check in on her and bring her each meal. During that time, Finn and Florian did a wonderful job of caring for Freedom, who was anxiously waiting in the stables to be reunited with Esme.

Headmaster Osgood's thoughts of expelling Esme from the academy were soon put to rest upon receiving an abundance of letters from grateful villagers, writing to him in praise of what Esme had done for them, and of how highly they thought of the academy. After holding several meetings with stakeholders in higher positions, the headmaster agreed that it was time for Dragon

Academy to refocus its position on how to approach the Sparkmasters.

In her three years at Dragon Academy, Esme went on to train with Freedom in a whole new range of classes. The teachers and students learnt together about how best to take on an enemy, all whilst at the heart of it, keeping dragon welfare in mind. Of course, the traditional classes continued, much to Esme's benefit. In them, she learned all about the different types of dragons. She loved learning about how water dragons took in energy from the rain, and of how star dragons were at their strongest by nightfall.

Following her graduation from Dragon Academy, Esme kept in touch, occasionally returning to give guest lectures on the history of how she came to have her first battle with the Sparkmasters. The battle was the first of many; the world would never be rid of Sparkmasters entirely, but through outreach programmes, the academy was able to engage with more people, educating them about dragons in hopes of being able to limit the Sparkmasters' scope to recruit more members.

Esme remains close friends with Finn, Florian and Felix to this very day. She can often be seen in flight upon Freedom's back, not just in battle, but for everyday journeys too. She often pays her parents a visit. They are always delighted to see her with Freedom, for they, and all the other villagers, now know that dragons are not to be feared, but celebrated and loved.

***